Dear Parent:

Congratulations! Your child is taking the first steps on an exciting journey. The destination? Independent reading!

STEP INTO READING® will help your child get there. The program offers five steps to reading success. Each step includes fun stories and colorful art. There are also Step into Reading Sticker Books, Step into Reading Math Readers, Step into Reading Phonics Readers, Step into Reading Write-In Readers, and Step into Reading Phonics Boxed Sets—a complete literacy program with something for every child.

Learning to Read, Step by Step!

Ready to Read Preschool–Kindergarten
• big type and easy words • rhyme and rhythm • picture clues
For children who know the alphabet and are eager to begin reading.

Reading with Help Preschool–Grade 1
• basic vocabulary • short sentences • simple stories
For children who recognize familiar words and sound out new words with help.

Reading on Your Own Grades 1–3
• engaging characters • easy-to-follow plots • popular topics
For children who are ready to read on their own.

Reading Paragraphs Grades 2–3
• challenging vocabulary • short paragraphs • exciting stories
For newly independent readers who read simple sentences with confidence.

Ready for Chapters Grades 2–4
• chapters • longer paragraphs • full-color art
For children who want to take the plunge into chapter books but still like colorful pictures.

STEP INTO READING® is designed to give every child a successful reading experience. The grade levels are only guides. Children can progress through the steps at their own speed, developing confidence in their reading, no matter what their grade.

Remember, a lifetime love of reading starts with a single step!

For Amanda Elliott,
teacher extraordinaire —J.L.

Step into Reading, Random House, and the Random House colophon are registered trademarks of Random House, Inc.

Visit us on the Web!
StepIntoReading.com
randomhousekids.com

Educators and librarians, for a variety of teaching tools, visit us at RHTeachersLibrarians.com

ISBN 978-0-7364-3660-1 (trade) — ISBN 978-0-7364-8189-2 (lib. bdg.)
ISBN 978-0-7364-3661-8 (ebook)

Printed in the United States of America   10 9 8 7 6 5 4 3 2 1

STEP INTO READING®

STEP 1 READY TO READ

DISNEY
PRINCESS

Princesses and Puppies

By Jennifer Liberts

Illustrated by Francesco Legramandi

Random House 🏠 New York

The Prince gives
Cinderella a puppy!

Cinderella's puppy
gives her kisses.

Who is hiding
in the flowers?

Rapunzel finds
a fluffy white puppy!

Rapunzel finds
the puppy's family.

Belle gets
to choose a puppy.

Belle picks
a wiggly puppy!

Merida sees a puppy.

He rolls in the mud.

Merida gives
the puppy a bath.
<u>Splash!</u>

A puppy wants
to play with Tiana.

The puppy naps
on Tiana's lap.

A puppy does a trick
for Jasmine!

Princesses love puppies!